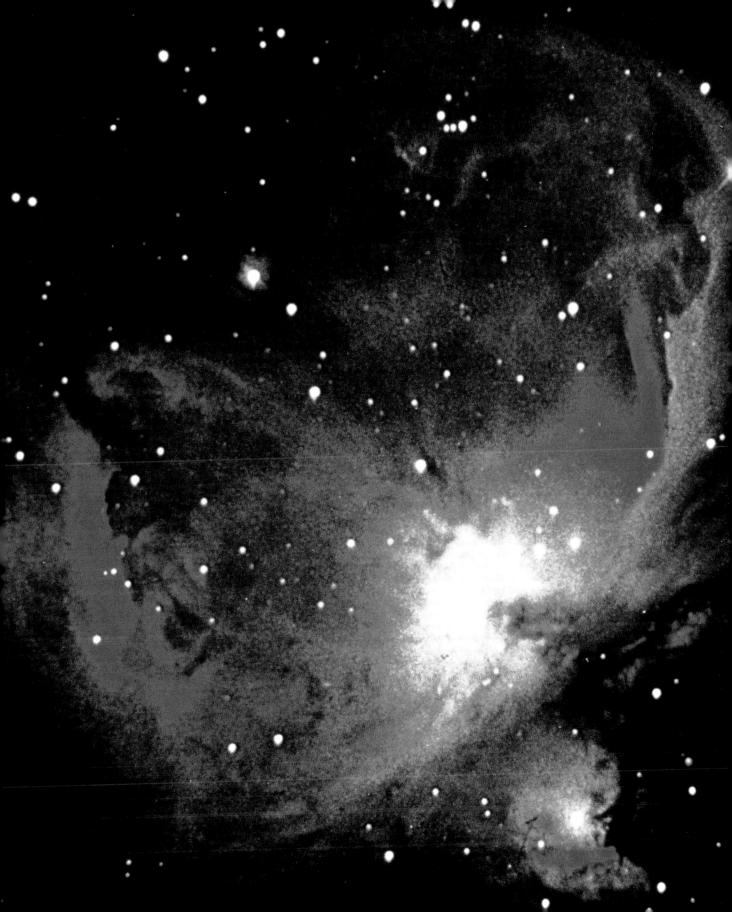

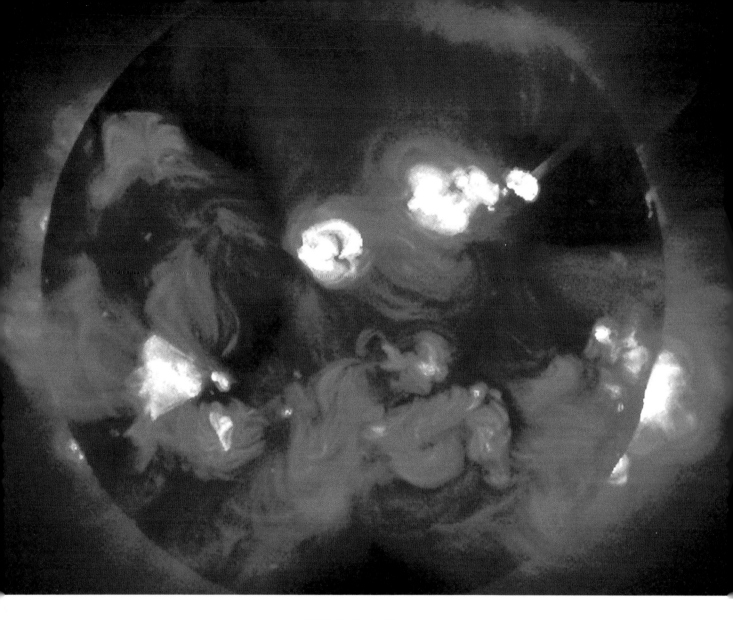

Published by Creative Education
123 South Broad Street, Mankato, Minnesota 56001
Creative Education is an imprint of The Creative Company

Art direction by Rita Marshall; Production design by The Design Lab

Photographs by NASA, Tom Stack & Associates (TSADO/ESO, TSADO/NASA)

Library of Congress Cataloging-in-Publication Data

George, Michael.
Stars / by Michael George.
p. cm. — (LifeViews)
ISBN 1-58341-250-6
1. Stars—Juvenile literature. 2. Astronomy—Juvenile literature.
I. Title. II. Series.

QB801.7 .G46   2003
523.8—dc21   2002034789

First Edition

2 4 6 8 9 7 5 3 1

BEACONS IN THE SKY
STARS

MICHAEL GEORGE

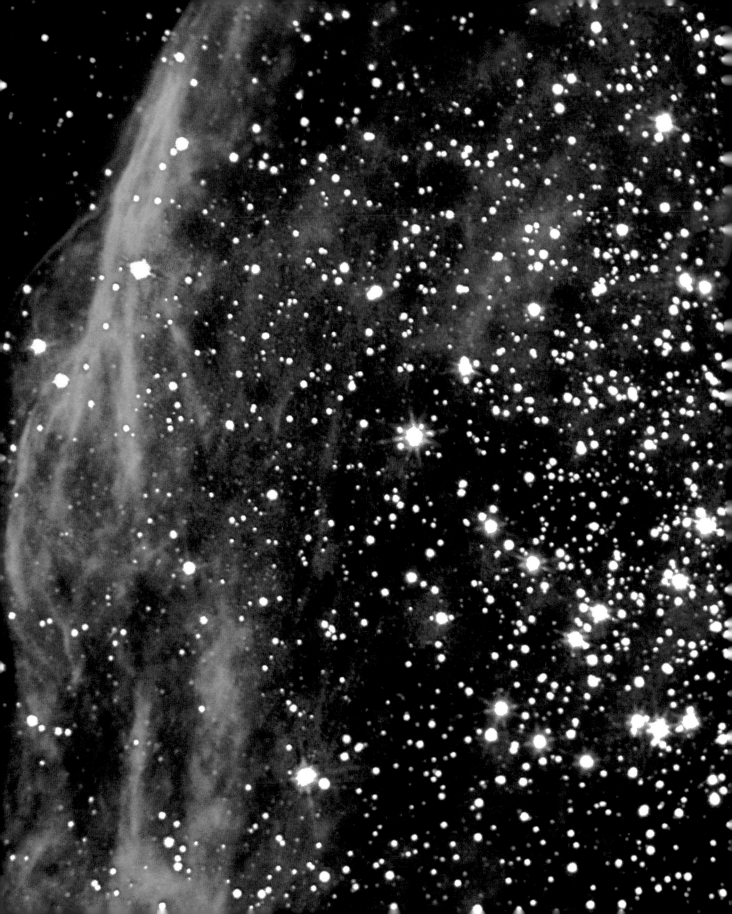

PEOPLE HAVE ALWAYS

been fascinated by the stars. Twinkling in the dark night sky, stars evoke questions that beg to be answered: What are stars? How far away are they? What is their significance for life on Earth? Over the past few centuries, scientists have answered many of these questions, and the answers reveal the intricate workings of our **universe** and the delicate balance of life on Earth.

Many people think that stars are visible only at night. One star, however, can be seen only during the day: the **sun**. The sun is an enormous ball of hot, glowing gases. It is large enough to hold more than one million Earths, and

The number of stars in the universe is endless.

hot enough to warm our **planet** and light our sky. Without the sun, Earth would be frozen, the sky would be black, and life as we know it would not exist on our planet.

Despite its unique appearance and importance to life on Earth, the sun is just an ordinary star. It is no different from the stars that are visible every night. The sun appears to be bigger and brighter than all the other stars simply because it is the closest star to Earth. Like the sun, all stars are extremely large, hot balls of glowing gas.

On dark, moonless nights, we can see about 2,000 stars in the sky. However, there are countless other stars that cannot be seen. In fact, many of the specks of light in the night sky are actually two stars. The stars in these pairs, called **binary stars**, circle around each other in space. Most binary stars appear to be single stars simply because they are so far away from Earth.

There are also many specks of light in the night sky that are actually three, four, or even more stars. These groups of stars are called multiple star systems. The largest star systems

Solar flares are sudden, short-lived bursts of light emitted from the sun's surface. The amount of energy released in each flare is equal to millions of hydrogen bombs exploding at once.

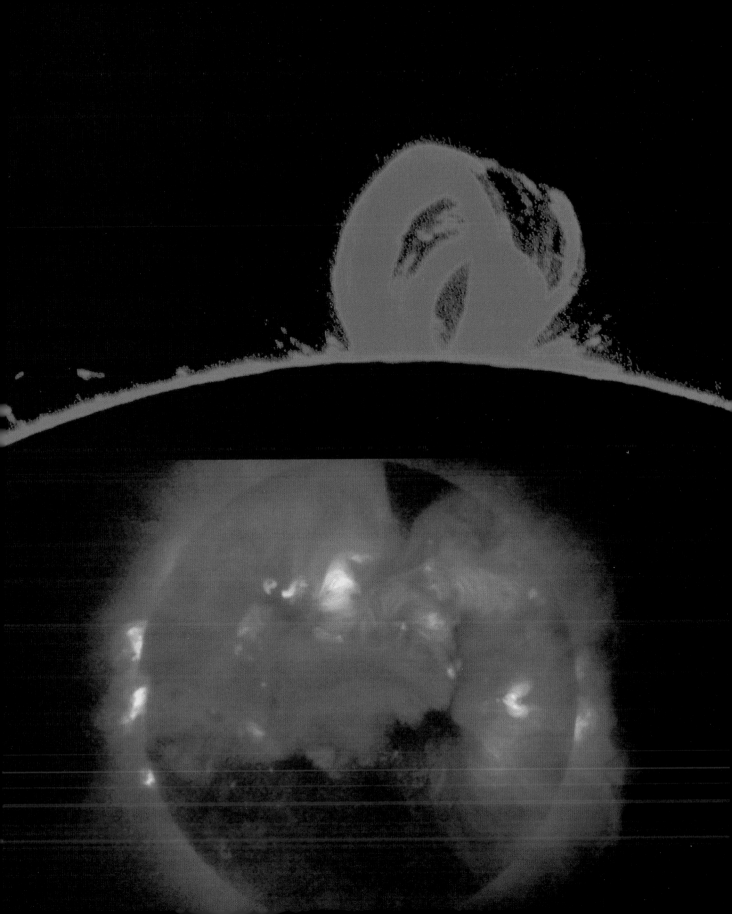

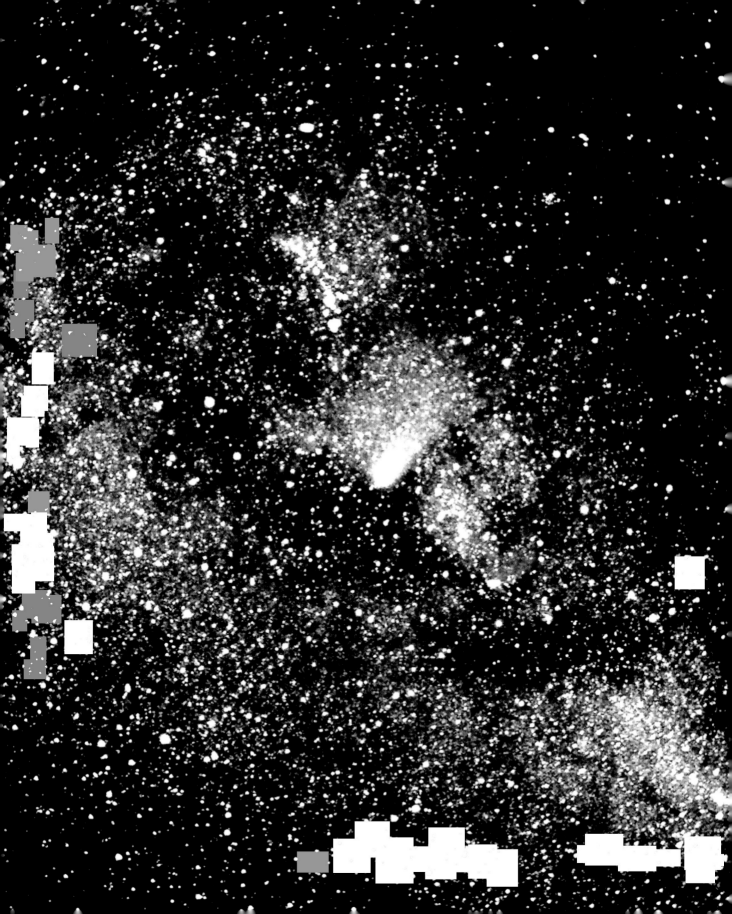

in the universe are called galaxies. Our solar system, which includes the sun, Earth, and the other eight planets, belongs to the **Milky Way** galaxy. The galaxy looks like a huge, hazy cloud stretching across the sky. A common telescope reveals that this cloud is a collection of billions of stars. Scientists estimate that the Milky Way galaxy contains 200 billion stars.

Although it is difficult to comprehend all the stars in our galaxy, the Milky Way is not the only galaxy in the universe. Peering between the stars in our galaxy, scientists can see other galaxies sprinkled throughout space. Scientists estimate that there are 100 billion galaxies in the universe, each containing an average of 100 billion stars. In all, there are as many stars in the universe as there are grains of sand on Earth.

Of all the stars in the universe, the sun is the closest star to Earth. However, the sun is still about 93 million miles (150 million km) away. If we traveled in the fastest spaceship

Last seen in 1986, Halley's Comet makes its orbit within the vast Milky Way galaxy. Comets are small, frozen masses of dust and gas that revolve around the sun. Halley's Comet will be visible again in 2061.

toward the sun, it would take many years to reach its surface.

The light that we see from the sun travels 187,000 miles (301,070 km) every second, or nearly 700 million miles (1.1 billion km) per hour. Although sunlight travels incredibly fast, it still takes some time for it to reach Earth. The light that we see from the sun has been traveling through space for just over eight minutes. These **rays** of light are actually images of the sun. Therefore, we do not see the sun as it is at this moment; we see an image of the sun as it was about eight minutes ago.

The stars we see in the night sky are millions of times farther away than the sun. The light we see from the star closest to the sun, called **Proxima Centauri**, left the surface more than four years ago. Therefore, we see Proxima Centauri as it was four years ago. Other stars are so far away that we see them as they were thousands of years ago, when our ancestors lived in caves. Some stars are even farther away than this. We see these stars as they were before life existed on Earth, or before Earth had even formed.

Space is filled with fascinating objects. Between 1758 and 1782, French astronomer Charles Messier cataloged 109 different objects, including galaxies, star clusters, and nebulae. His work still leads to new discoveries today.

Our planet changed drastically in the time it took the light from distant stars to reach it. Similarly, the stars have also changed. In fact, some of the stars we see in the sky may not even exist any longer. This is because stars, like people, are born and eventually die. During their lives, stars change in remarkable ways.

A star is born in a giant cloud of gas and dust called a nebula. Nebulae, the plural form of nebula, consist mainly of tiny hydrogen atoms, but contain other microscopic particles as well. Within some nebulae are small, dense balls of dust and gas called **globules**. Just as Earth's gravity pulls objects toward the ground, a globule's gravity pulls dust and gas toward its surface. Bit by bit, the globule grows in size. After millions of years, the globule is a dense, heavy globe, hundreds of times larger than Earth.

As the globule continues to grow, matter in the globule is packed closer and closer together. With the pressure constantly increasing, the temperature at the center of the globe begins to soar. Eventually, the core becomes hot

Nebulae either foster the formation of new stars or represent the end of a star's life. Some emit their own light, some are lit by nearby stars, and others, called dark nebulae, absorb light.

enough to set off a chain of **nuclear** explosions. In a process called nuclear fusion, hydrogen atoms combine to form a completely different atom called helium. Nuclear fusion releases tremendous amounts of **energy**, and the star begins to shine.

Once a star begins to shine, its surface churns with currents, turbulence, and gigantic waves of gas. Occasionally, thick clouds of glowing gas burst above the surface. As these blazing sheets of gas drift above the star, violent **storms** rage across the surface. These storms, called sunspots, look like dark patches because they are thousands of degrees cooler than the rest of the star. Sometimes, sunspots erupt with violent explosions that send streams of particles and radiation far into space.

As the surface of a star erupts with activity, nuclear fusion moves out from the center of the star toward fresh hydrogen fuel. Meanwhile, a growing core of helium ash is left behind. After about 10 billion years, most stars begin to run out of hydrogen fuel. With less energy flowing toward

First discovered in 1747, the Lagoon Nebula is a hotbed of new star formation. Because its gas and dust cloud is thin but widespread, Lagoon is classified as a diffuse nebula.

the surface, the star begins to contract. As the core of the star is squeezed tighter and tighter, the helium ash grows hotter and hotter. Eventually, the temperature becomes so hot that helium atoms begin to "melt" together, forming completely new atoms called **carbon**. This releases more energy and causes the star to burst, similar to a piece of popcorn.

Enlarged stars such as these are called **red giants**. Red giants are enormous stars, even when compared to the sun. Most are about 40 to 50 million miles (64–81 million km) across, or about 50 times wider than the sun. Some red giants are even larger than this. **Betelgeuse**, the red supergiant closest to the sun, is 250 million miles (403 million km) across. If Betelgeuse were in the place of the sun, it would engulf Mercury, Venus, Earth, and Mars.

Nuclear fusion cannot continue forever in the aging star. Eventually, most of the star's helium fuel is converted into carbon. Once again, the star begins to contract, and temperatures begin to rise. However, carbon atoms do not ignite easily. Soon, temperatures become so hot that the star

The Orion (left, right) and Horsehead (middle) Nebulae are parts of a much larger cloud of gas and dust that extends across more than half of the constellation Orion, to which Betelgeuse belongs.

explodes and hurls its outer layers of gas into space. The expanding cloud of gases, appearing round and planetlike, is a planetary nebula.

The remaining star, now called a **white dwarf**, shines dimly through the cloud of gas and dust. A white dwarf has no source of new energy but continues to glow simply because it is hot. Given time, the white dwarf loses heat into space and finally turns into a dark globe—a black dwarf.

Average-sized stars, such as the sun, follow the life cycle described above. Stars that are two or three times larger than the sun have a different fate. Under the crushing weight of a massive star, temperatures rise so high in the core that carbon atoms undergo nuclear fusion. They fuse together into a variety of other atoms. This releases additional energy for a time, but eventually, even a massive star runs out of fuel.

After all the nuclear fuel in a massive star has been used, the central core is crushed by the star's tremendous weight. This sets off a violent explosion called a **supernova**. A supernova makes the star millions of times brighter than normal and

Regions of star formation often appear red because of the reaction between the young stars' heat and the nebula's gas (mostly hydrogen). This type of nebula is called an emission nebula.

hurls the outer layers of the star into space. In some cases, the core of the star is also shattered. In other cases, the supernova leaves a tightly packed ball of matter called a **neutron star**.

Neutron stars are only 6 to 12 miles (10–19 km) across. Although they are very small, neutron stars contain more matter than the sun. A single drop of a neutron star would weigh billions of pounds on Earth. Like a white dwarf, a neutron star has no source of new energy and can only cool with time.

Stars that are 10 to 20 times larger than the sun end their lives in the most dramatic fashion of all. When a star this massive runs out of fuel, the tremendous gravity of the star causes it to collapse. As a star is packed tighter and tighter, the gravity of the star grows continuously stronger. Eventually the gravity is so strong that the star itself is crushed out of existence. All that remains is the star's intense gravitational field, known as a **black hole**.

The gravity of a black hole is so strong that nothing within a certain distance can resist its pull. A black hole can

Compared to globular star clusters (top), which are billions of years old, the Crab Nebula (bottom) is quite young, created by a supernova explosion in 1054. A special neutron star called a pulsar spins at its center.

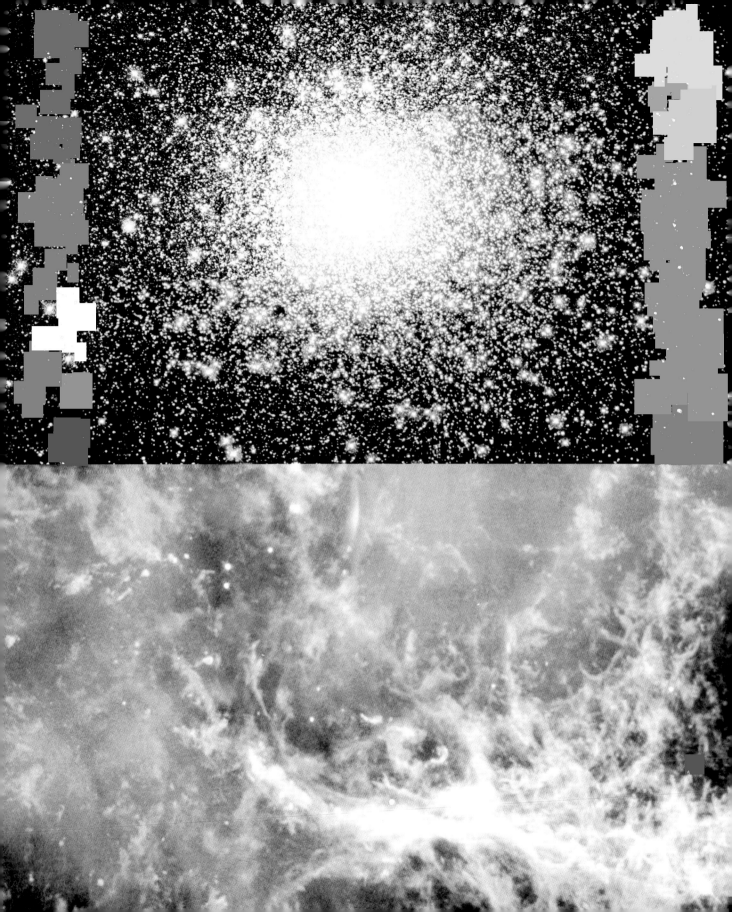

engulf stars, planets, and entire solar systems. Whatever enters a black hole is lost from this universe forever; nothing, not even a beam of light, can escape.

All stars change in dramatic ways. During their long lives, stars transform hydrogen into helium, helium into carbon, and carbon into a variety of other elements. In the last stages of their existence, stars hurl this newly formed matter into space. Once shed by a star, this material drifts through space as a thin cloud of gas and dust. Given time, it combines with the remains of other stars to form a nebula.

As we have learned, a nebula eventually condenses into a new star. Our sun is one of these newer stars. The nebula that condensed into the sun also formed Earth and the other planets in our solar system. This nebula contained carbon, **oxygen**, and all the other elements we now find on Earth. These elements, created long ago in

Like all stars, the sun (top, left) originated within a nebula (middle, right). Scientists believe that in about five billion years the sun will likely collapse, releasing its outer gases and becoming a white dwarf.

aging stars, are the basic building blocks of everything on Earth, including human beings. And so, in a way, we are all made of star dust.

Stars are more than just specks of light in the sky. Every star is an evolving ball of hot, glowing gases. During their long lives, stars create the elements from which the planets—and we ourselves—are made. The stars also hint at the **immensity** of our universe and suggest the vastness of time. The next time you stare into the night sky, consider infinity, consider time, and consider life.

No one knows whether life exists beyond the stars.

STARGAZING

When the ancient Greeks looked up into the sky more than 2,000 years ago, they saw many of the same stars we see today. They named patterns of bright stars, or constellations, after the objects, animals, or people they resembled. We still use these names today, names such as Ursa Major, the Great Bear; Orion, the Hunter; and Canis Major, the Great Dog. Astronomers currently use 88 constellations to map the sky. You can explore a few stars of the northern sky by following the instructions below.

You Will Need
- A magnetic compass
- A clear, dark night

Finding the North Star
1. Face north and try to find the Big Dipper. Made of seven bright stars within the constellation Ursa Major, the Big Dipper looks like a pan with a long handle. Depending upon the season, the handle may be pointing up, down, or sideways.
2. Locate the two bright stars farthest from the handle, called the pointers, and follow them north until you come to another bright star, Polaris, which is also called the North Star. More than 400 light-years from Earth, Polaris is the end star in the handle of the Little Dipper and lies almost directly above the North Pole.

Finding the Dog Star

Note: Orion is best viewed on a clear night in January or February, between 8 and 10 p.m.

1. Facing south, look into the sky at a point about 45 degrees above the horizon and try to find Orion. The Orion constellation consists of seven bright stars: two mark Orion's shoulders, two mark his knees, and three across the middle make up his belt. Betelgeuse, the bright, reddish star that marks Orion's right shoulder, is a red supergiant star. It is 300 times larger than the sun.

2. If you draw an imaginary line through Orion's belt downward, it points to Sirius, the brightest star in the sky. Sirius is part of the Canis Major constellation and is often called the Dog Star.

Observation

Because Earth is a sphere, the northern and southern hemispheres each have their own set of visible constellations. Someone in Australia, for example, will not be able to see the same constellations as someone in Canada—and vice versa. Stars also appear to shift position from season to season as Earth circles around the sun. The Big Dipper, for example, appears right-side up in the fall, but upside down in the spring.

OUR CLOSEST STAR

Even though it's 93 million miles (150 million km) from Earth, the sun is still our closest star. The next closest, called Proxima Centauri, is four light-years away. This means that light from the star takes four years to reach Earth. To visualize just how far that is, mark a dot on a piece of paper and label it "the sun." Then, measure about three and a quarter inches (5 cm), mark another dot, and label it "Earth." Using this distance ratio, Proxima Centauri would be about seven and a half miles (12 km) from your Earth dot!

The sun has been shining for roughly five billion years—and is expected to shine for another five billion. You should never look directly at the sun because, despite its distance, it can blind you. To safely study the sun, cover one lens of a pair of binoculars and point the binoculars at the sun—*without looking through them!* Position a piece of white cardboard behind the eyepiece so that the binoculars throw an image of the sun onto it. Dark spots on the image, called sunspots, represent cooler areas on the sun's surface.

LEARN MORE ABOUT STARS

The American Association of
    Amateur Astronomers
P.O. Box 7981
Dallas, TX 75209
http://www.corvus.com

Goddard Space Flight Center
Greenbelt Road
Greenbelt, MD 20771
http://www.gsfc.nasa.gov

NASA
Public Affairs Office - Code P
300 E Street SW
Washington, D.C. 20546
http://www.nasa.gov

Office of Public Outreach
Space Telescope Science Institute
3700 San Martin Drive
Baltimore, MD 21218
http://hubblesite.org

Space Center Houston
Johnson Space Center
1601 NASA Road
Houston, TX 77058
http://www.spacecenter.org

Space Environment Center R/SE
325 Broadway
Boulder, CO 80305
http://www.sec.noaa.gov

INDEX

The universe continues to fascinate, inspire, and humble us.